This book belongs to

ON
THE WAY
HOME

Jill Murphy

MACMILLAN CHILDREN'S BOOKS

Copyright © 1982 Jill Murphy

First published 1982 by Macmillan Children's Books
This edition reprinted 1997 by Macmillan Children's Books,
an imprint of Macmillan Publishers Limited,
a division of Macmillan Limited,
20 New Wharf Road, London N1 9RR
Basingstoke and Oxford
Associated companies worldwide
www.panmacmillan.com

15 14

ISBN 0 333 37572 6

A CIP catalogue for this book is available
from the British Library.

Printed in Hong Kong.

Claire had a bad knee, so she set off home to tell her mum all about it.

On the way home Claire met her friend Abigail.
"Look at my bad knee," said Claire.
"How did you do it?" asked Abigail.

"*Well*," said Claire, "there was a *very* big, bad wolf, and it

came sneaking up behind me as I passed by, and it tried to take me home

for its tea! But I screamed for help, and a woodcutter came and chased the

wolf away, and the wolf dropped me, and *that's* how I got my bad knee." "Gosh!" said Abigail.

Then Claire met her friend Paul.
"Look at my bad knee," said Claire.
"How did you do it?" asked Paul.

"*Well*," said Claire, "there was
a *vast* flying-saucer and

it came zooming out of the sky and tried to carry me off to a distant planet!

But I struggled free just in time and fell crashing to the earth far below,

and *that's* how I got my bad knee."   "Good gracious *me*!" gasped Paul.

Then Claire met her friend Amarjit.
"Look at my bad knee," said Claire.
"How did you do it?" asked Amarjit.

"*Well*," said Claire, "there was a huge, hungry crocodile,

and it came lumbering out of the canal as I passed by, and it tried to pull

me into the water! But I crammed a piece of wood between its jaws and it

was *so* cross that it knocked me over with its tail, and *that's* how I got my bad knee." "How dreadful!" said Amarjit.

Then Claire met her friend Robert.
"Look at my bad knee," said Claire.
"How did *you* do it?" asked Robert.

"*Well*," said Claire, "there was a big, fat snake, and it

came slithering out of a tree, and it wrapped itself around me and it

squeezed and **squashed**! But I tickled it until it couldn't stop laughing and

it dropped me, and *that's* how I got my bad knee." "I *say!*" gasped Robert.

Then Claire met her friend Samantha. "Look at my bad knee," said Claire. "How did you do it?" asked Samantha.

"*Well*," said Claire, "there was an enormous dragon, and

it came soaring out of the clouds and it picked me up in its claws! But I

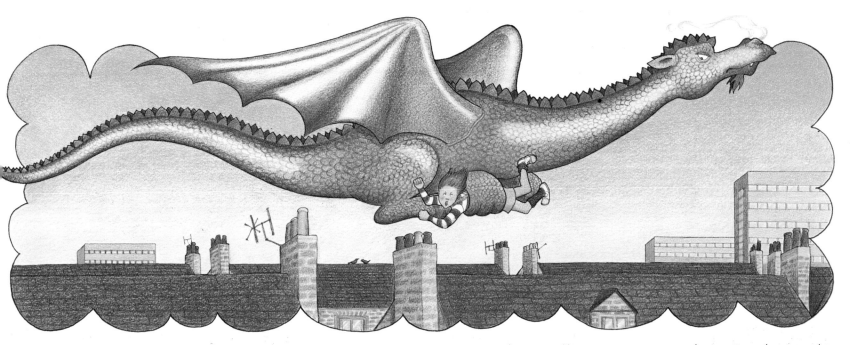

gave it such a big kick that it dropped me, and I fell for *miles* and *miles* through

the air, and *that's* how I got my bad knee."   "Cor!" cried Samantha.

Then Claire met her friend Nick. "Look at my bad knee," said Claire. "How did you do it?" asked Nick.

"*Well,*" said Claire, "there was a great, hairy gorilla, and

it came creeping out of a garage as I passed by and it tried to drag me

away! But I stamped on its toe *so* hard that it let me fall to the ground with a

bump, and *that's* how I got my bad knee, *and* I didn't cry. "   " Crumbs!" said Nick.

Then Claire met her friend Celia.
"Look at my bad knee," said Claire.
"How did you do it?" asked Celia.

"*Well*," said Claire, "there was a gigantic giant

and he came stamping through the houses, and he picked me up and said,

"Fee fie foe fum, a tasty girl for my hungry tum!" But I punched him on the nose

so hard that he let me
fall, and *that's* how I got my bad knee."

" Well I *never*! " exclaimed Celia.

Then Claire met her friend Jonathan.
"Look at my bad knee," said Claire.
"How did you do it?" asked Jonathan.

"*Well*," said Claire, "there was a ghastly ghost,

and it came gliding out of a gloomy graveyard as I passed by, and it went

'𝒲𝒪𝒪𝒪𝒪𝒪𝒪𝒪𝒪𝒪𝒪!' But I ran away *so* fast that I left it behind, and then

I tripped over, and *that's* how I got my bad knee." "Wow!" said Jonathan.

Then Claire met her friend Hannah.
"Look at my bad knee," said Claire.
"How did you do it?" asked Hannah.

"*Well*," said Claire, "there was a wicked old witch and she came

swooping down from the rooftops and bundled me into her shopping-bag!

But I broke the bag with my feet and dived out onto the hard pavement,

and *that's* how I got my bad knee."

"Dear me!" exclaimed Hannah.

Claire arrived home and her mum came out.
"Look at my bad knee," said Claire.
"How did you do it?" asked her mum.

" *Well*, "said Claire," I was in the playground and I was

having *such* a nice time on a swing when *suddenly*, *suddenly* ———

——————————————*I fell off !*" Claire burst into tears.

"Never mind," said her mum. "Come inside and we'll put a plaster on it."

"A very *big* plaster?" asked Claire.   "The biggest in the whole box," said her mum.

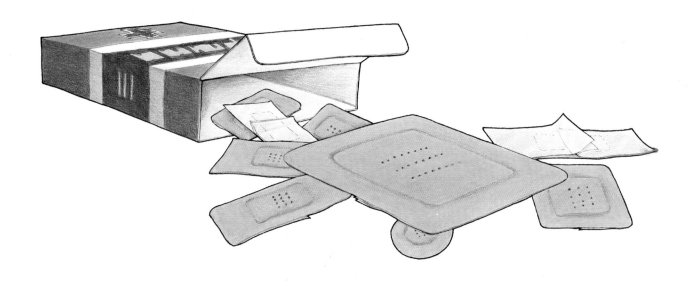

Other Macmillan picture books you will enjoy

Fruits Valerie Bloom and David Axtell
Charlie's Checklist Rory S. Lerman and Alison Bartlett
Peace at Last Jill Murphy
Sassy Gracie James Sage and Pierre Pratt
Picnic Farm Christine Morton and Sarah Barringer
The Pear Tree Meredith Hooper and Bee Willey